W. K. Clifford

Very short Stories and Verses for Children

W. K. Clifford

Very short Stories and Verses for Children

ISBN/EAN: 9783744750127

Printed in Europe, USA, Canada, Australia, Japan

Cover: Foto ©Andreas Hilbeck / pixelio.de

More available books at **www.hansebooks.com**

VERY SHORT STORIES

AND

VERSES FOR CHILDREN.

BY

Mrs. W. K. CLIFFORD,

AUTHOR OF " ANYHOW STORIES," &c.

With Illustrations by Edith Campbell.

LONDON:

WALTER SCOTT, 24 WARWICK LANE,

PATERNOSTER ROW.

1886.

Preface.

THESE stories, with the exception of the first one, are reprinted from two little books—"Children Busy," etc., and "Under Mother's Wing." They were then only signed with my initials. Some of the verses appear now for the first time. L. C.

TO YOU——AND ETHEL AND ALICE

CONTENTS.

MASTER WILLIE.

THERE was once a little boy called Willie. I never knew his other name, and as he lived far off behind the mountain, we cannot go to inquire. He had fair hair and blue eyes, and there was something in his face that, when you had looked at him, made you feel quite happy and rested, and think of all the things you meant to do by-and-by when you were wiser and stronger. He lived all alone with the tall aunt, who was very rich, in the big house at the end of the village. Every morning he went down the street with his little goat under his arm, and the village folk looked after him and said, "There goes Master Willie."

The tall aunt had a very long neck ; on the top of it was her head, on the top of her head she wore a white cap. Willie used often to look up at her and think that the cap was like snow upon the mountain. She was very fond of Willie, but she had lived a great many years and was always sitting still to think them over, and she had forgotten all the games she used to know, all the stories she had read when she was little, and when Willie asked her about them, would say, "No, dear, no, I can't remember ; go to the woods and play." Sometimes she would take his face between her two hands and look at him well while Willie felt quite sure that she was not thinking of him, but of someone else he did not know, and then she would kiss him, and turn away quickly, saying, " Go to the woods, dear ; it is no good staying with an old woman." Then he, knowing that she wanted to be alone, would pick up his goat and hurry away.

He had had a dear little sister, called Apple-blossom, but a strange thing had happened to her. One day she over-wound her very big doll that talked and walked, and the consequence was quite terrible. No sooner was the winding-up key out of the doll's side than it blinked its eyes, talked very fast, made faces, took Apple-blossom by the hand, saying, "I am not your doll any longer, but you are my little girl," and led her right away no one could tell whither, and no one was able to follow. The tall aunt and Willie only knew that she had gone to be the doll's little girl in some strange place, where dolls were stronger and more important than human beings.

After Apple-blossom left him, Willie had only his goat to play with ; it was a poor little thing with no horns, no tail and hardly any hair, but still he loved it dearly, and put it under his arm every morning while he went along the street.

"It is only made of painted wood and a little

hair, Master Willie," said the blacksmith's wife one day. "Why should you care for it; it is not even alive."

"But if it were alive, anyone could love it."

"And living hands made it," the miller's wife said. "I wonder what strange hands they were;— take care of it for the sake of them, little master."

"Yes, dame, I will," he answered gratefully, and he went on his way thinking of the hands, wondering what tasks had been set them to do since they fashioned the little goat. He stayed all day in the woods helping the children to gather nuts and blackberries. In the afternoon he watched them go home with their aprons full; he looked after them longingly as they went on their way singing. If he had had a father and mother, or brothers and sisters, to whom he could have carried home nuts and blackberries, how merry he would have been. Sometimes he told the children how happy they were to live in a cottage with the door open all day, and the sweet breeze blowing in, and the cocks and hens strutting about outside, and the pigs grunting in the styes at the end of the garden; to see the mother scrubbing and washing, to know that the father was working in the fields, and to run about and help and play, and be cuffed and kissed, just as it happened. Then they would answer, "But you have the tall lady for your aunt, and the big house to live in, and the grand carriage to drive in, while we are poor, and sometimes have little to eat and drink ; mother often tells us how fine it must be to be you."

"But the food that you eat is sweet because you are very hungry," he answered them, "and no one sorrows in your house.   As for the grand carriage, it is better to have a carriage if your heart is heavy, but when it is light, then you can run swiftly on your own two legs." Ah, poor Willie, how lonely he was, and yet the tall aunt loved him dearly. On hot drowsy days he had many a good sleep with his head resting against her high thin shoulders, and her arms about him.

One afternoon, clasping his goat as usual, he sat down by the pond.   All the children had gone home, so he was quite alone, but he was glad to look at the pond and think.   There were so many strange things in the world, it seemed as if he would never have done thinking about them, not if he lived to be a hundred.

He rested his elbows on his knees and sat staring at the pond.   Overhead the trees were whispering ; behind him, in and out of their holes the rabbits whisked; far off he could hear the twitter of a swallow ; the foxglove was dead, the bracken was turning brown, the cones from the fir trees were lying on the ground. As he watched, a strange thing happened.   Slowly and slowly the pond lengthened out and out, stretching away and away until it became a river —a long river that went on and on, right down the woods, past the great black firs, past the little cottage that was a ruin and only lived in now and then by a stray gipsy or a tired tramp, past the setting sun, till it dipped into space beyond. Then many little boats came sailing towards Willie, and one stopped quite close to where he sat, just as if it were waiting for him. He looked at it well; it had a snow-white sail and a little man with a drawn-sword for a figure-head. A voice that seemed to come from nowhere asked—

"Are you ready, Willie?" Just as if he understood he answered back—

"Not yet,—not quite, dear Queen, but I shall be soon. I should like to wait a little longer."

"No, no, come now, dear child; they are all waiting for you." So he got up and stepped into the boat, and it put out before he had even time to sit down. He looked at the rushes as the boat cut its way through them; he saw the hearts of the lilies as they lay spread open on their great wide leaves; he went on and on beneath the crimson sky towards the setting sun, until he slipped into space with the river.

He saw land at last far on a-head, and as he drew near it he understood whither the boat was bound. All along the shore there were hundreds and hundreds of dolls crowding down to the water's edge, looking as if they had expected him. They stared at him with their shining round eyes ; but he just clasped his little goat tighter and closer, and sailed on nearer and nearer to the land. The dolls did not move ; they stood still, smiling at him with their painted lips, then suddenly they opened their painted mouths and put out their painted tongues at him ; but still he was not afraid. He clasped the goat yet a little closer, and called out, "Apple-blossom, I am waiting ; are you here ?" Just as he had expected, he heard Apple-blossom's voice answering from the back of the toy-town—

"Yes, dear brother, I am coming." So he drew close to the shore, and waited for her. He saw her a long way off, and waved his hand.

"I have come to fetch you," he said.

"But I cannot go with you unless I am bought," she answered, sadly, "for now there is a wire spring inside me ; and look at my arms, dear brother ;" and pulling up her pink muslin sleeves, she showed him that they were stuffed with sawdust. "Go home, and bring the money to pay for me," she cried, "and then I can come home again." But the dolls had crowded up behind, so that he might not turn his boat round. "Straight on," cried Apple-blossom, in despair ; "what does it matter whether you go backwards or forwards if you only keep straight when you live in a world that is round ?"

So he sailed on once more beneath the sky that was getting grey, through all the shadows that gathered round, beneath the pale moon, and the little stars that came out one by one and watched him from the sky.

I saw him coming towards the land of story-books. That was how I knew about him, dear children. He was very tired and had fallen asleep, but the boat stopped quite naturally, as if it knew that I had been waiting for him. I stooped, and kissed his eyes, and looked at his little pale face, and lifting him softly in my arms, put him into this book to rest. That is how he came to be here for you to know. But in the toy-land Apple-blossom waits with the wire spring in her breast and the sawdust in her limbs ; and at home, in the big house at the end of the village, the tall aunt weeps and wails and wonders if she will ever see again the children she loves so well.

She will not wait very long, dear children. I know how it will all be. When it is quite dark to-night, and she is sitting in the leather chair with the high back, her head on one side, and her poor long neck aching, quite suddenly she will hear two voices shouting for joy. She will start up and listen, wondering how long she has been sleeping, and then she will call out—

"Oh, my darlings, is it you?" And they will answer back —

"Yes, it is us, we have come, we have come!" and before her will stand Willie and Apple-blossom. For the big doll will have run down, and the wire spring and the sawdust will have vanished, and Apple-blossom will be the doll's little girl no more. Then the tall aunt will look at them both and kiss them ; and she will kiss the poor little goat too, wondering if it is possible to buy him a new tail. But though she will say little, her heart will sing for joy. Ah, children, there is no song that is sung by bird or bee, or that ever burst from the happiest lips, that is half so sweet as the song we sometimes sing in our hearts—a song that is learnt by love, and sang only to those who love us.

SWINGING.

I.

SWING, swing, swing,
  Through the drowsy afternoon ;
Swing, swing, swing,
  Up I go to meet the moon.
Swing, swing, swing,
  I can see as I go high
Far along the crimson sky ;
  I can see as I come down
  The tops of houses in the town ;
  High and low,
  Fast and slow,
  Swing, swing, swing.

II.

Swing, swing, swing,
  See ! the sun is gone away ;
Swing, swing, swing,
  Gone to make a bright new day.
Swing, swing, swing.
  I can see as up I go
  The poplars waving to and fro,
  I can see as I come down
  The lights are twinkling in the town,
  High and low,
   Fast and slow,
  Swing, swing, swing.

THE WOODEN DOLL.

THE wooden doll had no peace. My dears, if ever you are a doll, hope to be a rag doll, or a wax doll, or a doll full of sawdust apt to ooze out, or a china doll easy to break—anything in the world rather than a good strong wooden doll with a painted head and movable joints, for that is indeed a sad thing to be. Many a time the poor wooden doll wished it were a tin train, or a box of soldiers, or a woolly lamb, or anything on earth rather than what it was. It never had any peace ; it was taken up and put down at all manners of odd moments, made to go to bed when the children went to bed, to get up when they got up, be bathed when they were bathed, dressed when they were dressed, taken out in all weathers, stuffed into their satchels when they went to school, left about in corners, dropped on stairs, forgotten, neglected, bumped, banged, broken, glued together,—anything and everything it suffered, until many a time it said sadly enough to its poor little self, " I might as well be a human being at once and be done with it !" And then it fell to thinking about human beings ; what strange creatures they were, always going about, though none carried them save when they were very little ; always sleeping and waking, and

eating and drinking, and laughing and crying, and
talking and walking, and doing this and that and
the other, never resting for long together, or seem-
ing as if they could be still for even a single day.
"They are always making a noise," thought the
wooden doll; "they are always talking and
walking about, always moving things and doing
things, building up and pulling down, and making
and unmaking for ever and for ever, and never are
they quiet. It is lucky that we are not all human
beings, or the world would be worn out in no time,
and there would not be a corner left in which to
rest a poor doll's head."

WATCHING.

DEAR father's ship is very near,
   We'll blow him kisses, baby dear,—
He may come home to-day.
A happy wind that journeys south
Seems just to linger round my mouth,
   Then bear a kiss away.

Come, baby, I will hold you—so,
We'll watch the waves that outward go,
   And call, "Come back to-day!"
For father's heart seems always near,
And who can tell but he may hear,
   Or know the words we say?

All round and up the cottage wall
The honeysuckle's grown so tall,
   It sees above the gate;
The flowers came hurrying up so sweet—
We told the little seeds they'd meet
   Dear father,—and they wait.

We first shall see a speck of white,
Far, far away, there where the light
   Has swept the morning dim;

So silent will his coming seem,
'Twill be like waking from a dream
   To wave our hands to him.

And then, and then he'll hoist you high,
And swiftly pass the people by,
   Just stopping here and there
To shake the neighbours by the hand,
And tell them of the southern land,
   And ask them how they fare.

He is not very far away,
For mother said he'd come to-day—
   We knew it by her face ;
She caught you up and kissed you so,
And now she's busy to and fro,
   And sings about the place.

THE LIGHT ON THE HILLS.

" I WANT to work at my picture," he said, and
went into the field. The little sister went
too, and stood by him watching while he painted.

"The trees are not quite straight," she said,
presently, "and oh, dear brother, the sky is not blue
enough."

"It will all come right soon," he answered.
"Will it be of any good?"

"Oh yes," she said, wondering that he should
even ask, " it will make people happy to look at it.
They will feel as if they were in the field."

"If I do it badly, will it make them unhappy?"

" Not if you do your very best," she answered ;
"for they will know how hard you have tried. Look
up," she said suddenly, "look up at the light upon
the hills," and they stood together looking at all
he was trying to paint, at the trees and the field,
at the deep shadows and the hills beyond, and
the light that rested upon them.

" It is a beautiful world," the girl said. " It is a
great honour to make things for it."

" It is a beautiful world," the boy echoed sadly.
"It is a sin to disgrace it with things that are
badly done."

" But you will do things well?"

"I get so tired," he said, "and long to leave off so much. What do you do when you want to do your best,—your very, very best?" he asked, suddenly.

"I think that I am doing it for the people I love," she answered. "It makes you very strong if you think of them ; you can bear pain, and walk far, and do all manner of things, and you don't get tired so soon."

He thought for a moment. "Then I shall paint my picture for you," he said ; "I shall think of you all the time I am doing it."

Once more they looked at the hills that seemed to rise up out of the deep shadows into the light, and then together they went home.

Soon afterwards a great sorrow came to the boy. While the little sister slept, she wandered into another world, and journeyed on so far that she lost the clue to earth, and came back no more. The boy painted many pictures before he saw the field again, but in the long hours, as he sat and worked, there came to him a strange power that answered more and more truly to the longing in his heart— the longing to put into the world something of which he was not ashamed, something which should make it, if only in the person of its meanest, humblest citizen, a little happier or better.

At last, when he knew that his eye was true and his touch sure, he took up the picture he had promised to paint for the dear sister, and worked at it until he was finished.

"This is better than all he has done before," the beholders said. "It is surely beautiful, for it makes one happy to look at it."

"And yet my heart ached as I did it," the boy said, as he went back to the field. "I thought of her all the time I worked,—it was sorrow that gave me power." It seemed as if a soft voice, that spoke only to his heart, answered back—

"Not sorrow but love, and perfect love has all things in its gift, and of it are all things born save happiness, and though that may be born too——"

"How does one find happiness?" interrupted the boy.

"It is a strange chase," the answer seemed to be ; "to find it for one's own self, one must seek it for others. We all throw the ball for each other."

"But it is so difficult to seize."

"Perfect love helps one to live without happiness," his own heart answered to himself ; "and above all things it helps one to work and to wait."

"But if it gives one happiness too?" he asked eagerly.

"Ah, then it is called Heaven."

WRITING A BOOK.

"LET us write a book," they said; "but what shall it be about?"

"A fairy story," said the elder sister.

"A book about kings and queens," said the other.

"Oh, no," said the brother, "let's write about animals."

"We will write about them all," they cried together. So they put the paper, and pens, and ink ready. The elder sister took up a fairy story and looked at it, and put it down again.

"I have never known any fairies," she said, "except in books; but, of course, it would not do to put one book inside another—anyone could do that."

"I shall not begin to-day," the little one said, "for I must know a few kings and queens before I write about them, or I may say something foolish."

"I shall write about the pig, and the pony, and the white rabbit," said the brother; "but first I must think a bit. It would never do to write a book without thinking."

Then the elder sister took up the fairy story again, to see how many things were left out, for those, she thought, would do to go into her book.

The little one said to herself, " Really, it is no good thinking about kings and queens until I have known some, so I must wait ; " and while the brother was considering about the pig, and the pony, and the white rabbit, he fell asleep.

So the book is not written yet, but when it is we shall know a great deal.

THE RABBIT.

THE moon is shining o'er the field,
  A little breeze is blowing,
The radish leaves are crisp and green,
  The lettuces are growing.

The owl is in the ivy-bush,
  With both his eyes a-winking ;
The rabbit shakes his little tail,
  And sits him down a-thinking—

" Oh ! where are all the dormice gone ?
  And are the frogs a-wooing ?
Will no one come to play with me ?
  What are they all a-doing ? "

Poor little rabbit, all alone,
  Don't let the master meet you ;
He'll shoot you with his little gun,
  And merrily he'll eat you !

THE SANDY CAT.

THE sandy cat sat by the kitchen fire. Yesterday it had had no supper; this morning everyone had forgotten it. All night it had caught no mice; all day as yet it had tasted no milk. A little grey mouse, a saucerful of milk, a few fish or chicken bones, would have satisfied it; but no grey mouse, with its soft stringy tail behind it, ran across the floor; no milk was near, no chicken bones, no fish, no anything. The serving-maid had been washing clothes, and was hanging them out to dry. The children had loitered on their way to school, and were wondering what the master would say to them. The father had gone to the fair to help a neighbour to choose a horse. The mother sat making a patchwork quilt. No one thought of the sandy cat; it sat by the fire alone and hungry.

At last the clothes were all a-drying, the children had been scolded, and sat learning a lesson for the morrow. The father came from the fair, and the patchwork quilt was put away. The serving-maid put on a white apron with a frill, and a clean cap, then taking the sandy cat in her arms, said, "Pussy, shall we go into the garden?" So they went and walked up and down, up and down the pathway, till at last they stopped before a rose tree;

the serving-maid held up the cat to smell the roses, but with one long bound it leaped from her arms and away—away—away.

Whither?

Ah, dear children, I cannot tell, for I was not there to see ; but if ever you are a sandy cat you will know that it is a terrible thing to be asked to smell roses when you are longing for a saucerful of milk and a grey mouse with a soft stringy tail.

ON THE WAY TO THE SUN.

HE had journeyed a long way, and was very tired. It seemed like a dream when he stood up after a sleep in the field, and looked over the wall, and saw the garden, and the flowers, and the children playing all about. He looked at the long road behind him, at the dark wood and the barren hills; it was the world to which he belonged. He looked at the garden before him, at the big house, and the terrace, and the steps that led down to the smooth lawn—it was the world which belonged to the children.

"Poor boy," said the elder child, "I will get you something to eat."

"But where did he come from?" the gardener asked.

"We do not know," the child answered; "but he is very hungry, and mother says we may give him some food."

"I will take him some milk," said the little one; in one hand she carried a mug and with the other she pulled along her little broken cart.

"But what is he called?" asked the gardener.

"We do not know," the little one answered; "but he is very thirsty, and mother says we may give him some milk."

"Where is he going?" asked the gardener.

"We do not know," the children said; "but he is very tired."

When the boy had rested well, he got up saying, "I must not stay any longer," and turned to go on his way.

"What have you to do?" the children asked.

"I am one of the crew, and must help to make the world go round," he answered.

"Why do we not help too?"

"You are the passengers."

"How far have you to go?" they asked.

"Oh, a long way!" he answered. "On and on until I can touch the sun."

"Will you really touch it?" they said, awestruck.

"I dare say I shall tire long before I get there," he answered sadly. "Perhaps without knowing it, though, I shall reach it in my sleep," he added. But they hardly heard the last words, for he was already far off.

"Why did you talk to him?" the gardener said. "He is just a working boy."

"And we do nothing! It was very good of him to notice us," they said, humbly.

"Good!" said the gardener in despair. "Why, between you and him there is a great difference."

"There was only a wall," they answered. "Who set it up?" they asked curiously.

"Why, the builders, of course.   Men set it up."

"And who will pull it down?"

"It will not want any pulling down," the man answered grimly.   "Time will do that."

As the children went back to their play, they looked up at the light towards which the boy was journeying.

"Perhaps we too shall reach it some day," they said.

IN THE MOONLIGHT.

H E picked a buttercup, and held it up to her chin. "Do you like butter?" he asked.

"Butter!" she exclaimed. "They are not made into butter. They are made into crowns for the Queen; she has a new one every morning."

"I'll make you a crown," he said. "You shall wear it to-night."

"But where will my throne be?" she asked.

"It shall be on the middle step of the stile by the corn-field."

So when the moon rose I went out to see.

He wore a red jacket and his cap with the feather in it. Round her head there was a wreath of buttercups; it was not much like a crown. On one side of the wreath there were some daisies, and on the other was a little bunch of blackberry-blossom.

"Come and dance in the moonlight," he said; so she climbed up and over the stile, and stood in the corn-field holding out her two hands to him. He took them in his, and then they danced round and round all down the pathway, while the wheat nodded wisely on either side, and the poppies awoke and wondered. On they went, on and on through the corn-field towards the broad green meadows stretching far into the distance. On and on, he shouting for joy, and she laughing out so merrily that the sound travelled to the edge of the wood, and the thrushes heard, and dreamed of Spring. On they went, on and on, and round and round, he in his red jacket, and she with the wild flowers dropping one by one from her wreath. On and on in the moonlight, on and on till they had danced all down the corn-field, till they had crossed the green meadows, till they were hidden in the mist beyond.

That is all I know ; but I think that in the far far off somewhere, where the moon is shining, he and she still dance along a corn-field, he in his red jacket, and she with the wild flowers dropping from her hair.

THE POOR LITTLE DOLL.

IT was a plain little doll that had been bought for sixpence at a stall in the market-place. It had scanty hair and a weak composition face, a calico body and foolish feet that always turned inwards instead of outwards, and from which the sawdust now and then oozed. Yet in its glass eyes there was an expression of amusement; they seemed to be looking not at you but through you, and the pursed-up red lips were always smiling at what the glass eyes saw.

"Well, you *are* a doll," the boy said, looking up from his French exercise. "And what are you staring at me for—is there anything behind?" he asked, looking over his shoulder. The doll made no answer. "And whatever are you smiling for?" he asked; "I believe you are always smiling. I believe you'd go on if I didn't do my exercise till next year, or if the cat died, or the monument tumbled down." But still the doll smiled in silence, and the boy went on with his exercise. Presently he looked up again and yawned. "I think I'll go for a stroll," he said, and put his book by. "I know what I'll do," he said, suddenly; "I'll take that doll and hang it up to the apple tree to scare away the sparrows." And calling out, "Sis, I have taken your doll ; I'm going to make a scarecrow of it," he went off to the garden.

His sister rushed after him, crying out, " Oh, my poor doll ! oh, my dear little doll !   What are you doing to it, you naughty boy ? "

" It's so ugly," he said.

" No, it is not ugly," she cried.

" And it's so stupid,—it never does anything but smile,—it can't even grow,—it never gets any bigger."

" Poor darling doll," Sis said, as she got it once more safely into her arms, " of course you can't grow, but it is not your fault, they did not make any tucks in you to let out."

" And it's so unfeeling. It went smiling away like anything when I could not do my French."

" It has no heart.   Of course it can't feel."

" Why hasn't it got a heart ? "

" Because it isn't alive. You ought to be sorry for it, and very, very kind to it, poor thing."

" Well, what is it always smiling for ? "

" Because it is so good," answered Sis, bursting into tears.   " It is never bad-tempered ; it never complains, and it never did anything unkind," and, kissing it tenderly, " you are always good and sweet," she said, " and always look smiling, though you must be very unhappy at not being alive."

THE VIOLETS.

THE sun came out and shone down on the leafless trees that cast hardly any shadows on the pathway through the woods.

"Surely the Spring is coming," the birds said; "it must be time to wake the flowers."

The thrush, and the lark, and the linnet sang sweetly. A robin flew up from the snow, and perched upon a branch; a little ragged boy at the end of the wood stopped and listened.

"Surely the Spring is coming," he too said; "and mother will get well."

The flowers that all through the Winter had been sleeping in the ground heard the birds, but they were drowsy, and longed to sleep on. At last the snowdrops came up and looked shiveringly about; and a primrose leaf peeped through the ground, and died of cold. Then some violets opened their blue eyes, and, hidden beneath the tangle of the wood, listened to the twittering of the birds. The little ragged boy came by; he saw the tender flowers, and, stooping down, gathered them one by one, and put them into a wicker basket that hung upon his arm.

"Dear flowers," he said, with a sigh, as if loth to pick them, "you will buy poor mother some breakfast," and, tying them up into little bunches, he carried them to the town. All the morning he stood by the road-side, offering his flowers to the passers-by, but no one took any notice of him; and his face grew sad and troubled. "Poor mother!" he said, longingly; and the flowers heard him, and sighed.

"Those violets are very sweet," a lady said as she passed; the boy ran after her.

"Only a penny," he said, "just one penny, for mother is at home." Then the lady bought them, and carried them to the beautiful house in which she lived, and gave them some water, touching them so softly that the poor violets forgot to long for the woods, and looked gratefully up into her face.

"Mother," said the boy, "see, I have brought some bread for your breakfast. The violets sent it to you," and he put the little loaf down before her.

The birds knew nothing of all this, and went on singing till the ground was covered with flowers, till the leaves had hidden the brown branches of the trees, and the pathway through the woods was all shade, save for the sunshine that flecked it with light.

THE FIDDLER.

THE fiddler played upon his fiddle
   All through that leafy June,
He always played hey-diddle-diddle,
   And played it out of tune.

And down the hill the children came,
   And down the valley too :
I never heard the fiddler's name,
   So cannot tell it you.
   Hey-diddle-diddle, diddle-diddle-dee.

On—on they came, and when they heard
   That tune so swift and sweet,
They did not say a single word,
   But shuffled with their feet.

Then round they went, and round and round,
   All to that cracked old fiddle,
And still was heard the magic sound,
   Hey-diddle-diddle-diddle,
   Hey-diddle-diddle, diddle-diddle-dee.

THE BROKEN HORSE.

THEY were all very sad, and the girl in the pink frock was crying bitterly, for they had been to the woods, and on the way home the wooden horse had fallen over on one side and broken off his head.

"Don't cry so, pray don't cry so," the little one said, as she knelt down in front of her sister, and tried to kiss her.

"And oh, sister," said the brother, "it would have been far worse if he had lost his tail too. Besides, perhaps he does not mind much; it is not as if he were alive."

"Ah, yes," sobbed the tall girl. "But when you are as old as I am you will know that it is a terrible thing to lose your head, even if it is only wooden."

THE RAINBOW-MAKER.

THE children stood under an archway. Behind them was the blue sky ; in front of them the clear, still lake that wandered and wound about the garden ; above their heads the leaves of a tree whispered and told strange stories to the breeze.

"Poor tree ! it is sighing for the blossoms the wind has carried away," they said to each other, and they looked back at the garden. "And, poor flowers, too," they said, "all your bright colours are gone, and your petals lie scattered on the ground ; to-morrow they will be dead." "Ah, no," the flowers sighed, "the rainbow-maker will gather them up, and once more they will see the sun." Before the children could answer, a tall fair maiden came down the pathway. They could see her plainly in the twilight. Her eyes were dim with gathering tears, but on her lips there was a smile that came and went and flickered round her mouth. All down her back hung her pale golden hair ; round her neck was a kerchief of many colours ; her dress was soft and white, and her snowy apron was gathered up in one hand. She looked neither to the right nor to the left. She did not utter a single word ; and the children could hear no sound of her footstep, no rustling from her dress. She stooped, and picking up the fading petals, looked at them tenderly for a moment, while the tears fell slowly down her cheeks ; but the smile hovered round her mouth ; for she knew that they would shine again in the sight of their beloved sun.   When her apron was quite full, she turned round and left the garden. Hand-in-hand the children followed.   She went slowly on by the side of the lake, far, far away across the meadows and up the farthest hill, until at last she found her home behind a cloud just opposite the sun.   There she sat all through the summer days making rainbows.   When the children had watched her for a long long time, they went softly back to their own home.   The rainbow-maker had not even seen them.

"Mother," they said one day, "we know now where the colours go from the flowers.   See, they are there," and as they spoke they thought of the maiden sitting silently at work in her cloud-home. They knew that she was weeping at sending forth her most beautiful one, and yet smiling as she watched the soft archway she had made.   "See, they are all there, dear mother," the children repeated, looking at the falling rain and the shining sun, and pointing to the rainbow that spanned the river.

OVER THE PORRIDGE.

THEY sat down to eat their porridge. The naughty little girl turned her back upon her sister, and put a large spoonful into her mouth.

"Oh—oh—oh!" she cried, "I have burnt my tongue."

"Eat it slowly," said the good little sister. *She* took up her porridge carefully, and after blowing it very gently, and waiting for a minute or two while it cooled, ate it, and found it very nice.

"I shall not eat mine until it is quite cold," said Totsey, getting cross.

"Then it will be nasty," said the good little sister, still going on with her own porridge.

"Oh, dear," said Totsey, "if I eat it too hot it burns me, and if I eat it too cold it's nasty. What shall I do?"

"Take it as I do mine," said the good little sister. "It is the right way."

"There are two wrong ways and only one right way; it isn't fair," sighed the naughty little girl. "And, oh! my porridge is so nasty." Then she asked, "Did you ever eat your porridge too hot and burn your tongue?"

"No," answered the good little sister; "I never ate my porridge too hot and burnt my tongue."

"Did you ever eat your porridge when it was quite cold and very nasty?"

"No," answered the good little sister again; "I never ate my porridge when it was quite cold and very nasty."

"Well, I have," said Totsey; "and so I know about two things that you do not know about." And the naughty little sister got up and walked away, and the good little sister sat still and thought about many things.

A-COMING DOWN THE STREET.

I.

THE baby she has golden hair,
　　Her cheeks are like a rose,
And she sits fastened in her chair,
　　A-counting of her toes.
The mother she stands by the door,
　　And all the place is neat,
She says, " When it is half-past four,
　　He'll come along the street."
And O ! in all this happy world
　　There's not a sight so sweet,
As 'tis to see the master, dear,
　　A-coming down the street.
　　　　A-coming O ! a-coming O !
　　　　A-coming down the street.

II.

The baby's sister toddles round,
　　And sings a little song,
And every word and every sound
　　Says, " Father won't be long."
And when he comes we'll laugh for glee,
　　And then his bonnie face,

However dark the day may be,
　Makes sunshine in the place.
And O ! in all this happy world
　There's not a sight so sweet,
As 'tis to see the master, dear,
　A-coming down the street,
　　A-coming O ! a-coming O !
　　A-coming down the street.

THE PROUD BOY.

THERE was once a very proud boy. He always walked through the village with his eyes turned down and his hands in his pockets. The boys used to stare at him, and say nothing ; and when he was out of sight, they breathed freely. So the proud boy was lonely, and would have had no friends out of doors if it had not been for two stray dogs, the green trees, and a flock of geese upon the common.

One day, just by the weaver's cottage, he met the tailor's son. Now the tailor's son made more noise than any other boy in the village, and when he had done anything wrong he stuck to it, and said he didn't care ; so the neighbours thought that he was very brave, and would do wonders when he came to be a man, and some of them hoped he would be a great traveller, and stay long in distant lands. When the tailor's son saw the proud boy he danced in front of him, and made faces, and provoked him sorely, until, at last, the proud boy turned round and suddenly boxed the ears of the tailor's son, and threw his hat into the road. The tailor's son was surprised, and, without waiting to pick up his hat, ran away, and sitting down in the carpenter's yard, cried bitterly. After a few minutes, the proud boy came to him and returned him his hat, saying politely—

"There is no dust on it ; you deserved to have your ears boxed, but I am sorry I was so rude as to throw your hat on to the road."

"I thought you were proud," said the tailor's son, astonished ; "I didn't think you'd say that—I wouldn't."

"Perhaps you are not proud?"

"No, I am not."

"Ah, that makes a difference," said the proud boy, still more politely. "When you are proud, and have done a foolish thing, you make a point of owning it."

"But it takes a lot of courage," said the tailor's son.

"Oh, dear, no," answered the proud boy ; "it only takes a lot of cowardice not to ;" and then turning his eyes down again, he softly walked away.

SEEKING THE VIOLETS.

ALL the wood had been blue with violets, but now they were nearly gone. The birds sang louder and louder to keep them and to call them back, but soon there was not a violet left in all the wood from end to end. The snowdrops died, and the primrose faded, the cowslips and blue-bells vanished, the thorn grew white with blossom, the wild honeysuckle filled the wood with its fragrance, and soon the fruit began to ripen.

The blackbirds and the swallows and the chaffinches, and all the birds they knew, gathered round the garden trees and bushes, and forgot the woods, until suddenly one day they espied a little child. She was sitting on a chair under a tree ; she had a little table before her and a pink ribbon round her hat ; she was eating fruit with a large silver spoon. The birds were afraid, and held aloof until a sparrow chirped and the child looked up, and when they saw how blue her eyes were, they sang out bravely and fluttered round her, thinking that she had brought them news from the violets. But she never looked up again, though the birds crowded on to the branch above her, and perched upon the table, and rubbed their little beaks against her plate. She just held on her hat with one hand,

and with the other went on taking up fruit with a silver spoon.

"Ah, dear child," a swallow twittered, "perhaps you do not know what is written in your eyes ; so many of us carry secrets that we ourselves know last of all."

TOMMY'S STOCKINGS.

TWO little maids went out one day,
    And really it was shocking !
They met poor Tommy on the way,
    With holes in either stocking.

They sat down on a low stone seat,
    And to and fro kept rocking,
While they knitted, swift and neat,
    Each of them a stocking.

And sweet they sang a little song,
    The dickie-birds kept mocking ;
And Tommy wished that all day long
    They'd sit and knit a stocking.

MIDSUMMER-NIGHT.

THE children were very much puzzled what to do, for it was Midsummer-night, and they knew that there was a dream belonging to it ; but how to come across it they could not tell. They knew that the dream had something to do with fairies, a queen, and all manner of lovely things ; but that was all. At first they thought they would sit up with the doors and windows open, and the dog on the steps ready to bark if he saw anything unusual. Then they felt sure that they could not dream while they were wide-awake, so three of them went to bed, and one dozed in a corner of the porch, with her clothes on. Presently the dog barked, and two children in their night-gowns ran out to see, and one took off her night-cap and looked out of window ; but it was only old Nurse coming back from a long gossip with the village black-smith's wife and mother-in-law. So the dog looked foolish, and Nurse was angry, and put them all to bed without any more ado.

"Oh," they cried, "but the fairies, and the queen, and the flowers ! What shall we do to see them ?"

" Go to sleep," said Nurse, "and the dream may come to you ;—you can't go to a dream," she added, for you see she was just a peasant woman, and had never travelled far, or into any land but her own.

So the children shut their eyes tightly and went to sleep, and I think that they saw something, for their eyes were very bright next morning, and one of them whispered to me, softly, " The queen wore a wreath of flowers last night, dear mother, and, oh, she was very beautiful."

THE LITTLE MAID.

A LITTLE maid went to market,
  'She went into the town,
And all the things she had to buy
  She carefully wrote down.
The coffee, sugar, tea, and rice—
  The currant cake for tea,
And then she had to reckon up,
  And see how much they'd be.

She sat her down as she came back,
  She sat her down to see
What they had cost—the currant cake,
  The coffee, and the tea.
She could not make her money right,
  And yet, how she did try !
She could not make her money right,
  And oh ! how she did cry.

She's counting still, my dears, my dears,
  She's counting day and night,
But though she counts for years and years,
  She'll never make it right.
She'll never make it right—right—right,
  Oh ! never any more,   [count,
Though she sits counting—count—count—
  Till she is ninety-four.

WAR

" I DON'T like you," said he, in a rage.

"You are a naughty boy," said she, crossly.

" I shall never speak to you again."

" I shall never play with you any more."

" I don't care."

"And I don't care."

" I shall tell of you."

"All right. I shall tell of you."

" Nasty mean thing to threaten."

" You threatened first."

" Nasty, disagreeable thing.",

" Ugly, unkind boy." Then they turned back to back, and stood sulking. He put his hands into his pockets, and she sucked her finger.

"That's the worst of a girl," thought he; " I shan't give in."

" I can't bear boys," thought she; " and I won't make it up to-day."

" We might have had good fun all this afternoon if she hadn't been so silly," he thought presently.

" It would have been so nice if he hadn't been disagreeable," she thought after a bit. Then he began to fidget and to kick the floor a little with one foot, and she began to cry and to wipe her tears away very softly and quickly, so that he might not see them.

PEACE.

HE looked over his shoulder quickly. She saw him, and turned still more quickly away. "I shall go and take a long walk in the woods," he said.

"You don't know where the rabbit-holes are," she answered.

"Yes, I do ; I found them out the other day."

"I shall go out with Mary."

"All right."

"And I shall never go into the woods with you any more."

"Very well. I don't care," he said. Then she broke down and sobbed.

"You are a very unkind boy."

"It's all your fault."

"No, it's all yours. You began."

"No, you began."

"You don't like me now," she sobbed.

"Yes, I do."

"You said I was a nasty, disagreeable thing."

"Well, I didn't mean it if I did. You said I was an ugly, unkind boy."

"Oh, but I didn't mean it," she said.

"You know I'm very fond of you."

"So am I of you."

"All right, then, let's make it up." So he turned round quickly and she turned round slowly, and he put his arms round her waist, and she put her hands up on to his shoulders, and they kissed each other, and hugged each other, and rubbed noses, and laughed.

"Shall we go to the woods?" she asked, doubtfully.

"Yes, come along."

"You said you'd go without me," she pouted.

"Oh, but I shouldn't have liked it a bit."

"And I should have been so unhappy," she said.

"And now we just will have a game," he answered, as hand-in-hand they went off as fast as they could scamper.

MY LITTLE BROTHER.

MY baby brother's fat, as fat
    As any boy can be,
And he is just the sweetest duck
    That ever you did see.

I count the dimples in his hands
    A dozen times a·day,
And often wonder when he coos
    What he would like to say.

I comb the down upon his head—
    He has'nt any hair,—
It must be cold without, and yet
    He never seems to care.

It is so nice to see him kick,
    He has such pretty feet ;
I think if we might eat him up
    It would be quite a treat.

THE KITE.

IT was the most tiresome kite in the world, always wagging its tail, shaking its ears, breaking its string, sitting down on the tops of houses, getting stuck in trees, entangled in hedges, flopping down on ponds, or lying flat on the grass, and refusing to rise higher than a yard from the ground.

I have often sat and thought about that kite, and wondered who its father and mother were. Perhaps they were very poor people, just made of newspaper and little bits of common string knotted together, obliged to fly day and night for a living, and never able to give any time to their children or to bring them up properly. It was pretty, for it had a snow-white face, and pink and white ears; and, with these, no one, let alone a kite, could help being pretty. But though the kite was pretty, it was not good, and it did not prosper; it came to a bad end, oh ! a terrible end indeed. It stuck itself on a roof one day, a common red roof with a broken chimney and three tiles missing. It stuck itself there, and it would not move ; the children tugged and pulled and coaxed and cried, but still it would not move. At last they fetched a ladder, and had nearly reached it when suddenly the kite started and flew away—right away over the field and over the heath, and over the far far woods, and it never came back again—never—never.

Dear, that is all. But I think sometimes that perhaps beyond the dark pines and the roaring sea the kite is flying still, on and on, farther and farther away, for ever and for ever.

THE TINKER'S MARRIAGE.

TWO beaux and a belle, a goat and a carriage,
    They all set off to the tinker's marriage.
Two three-cornered hats, and one with a feather,
They looked very fine in the sweet summer weather
But the carriage turned over, the poor goat shied,
The little belle laughed, the silly beaux cried,
And the tinker fumed, " Oh, why do they tarry?
And why don't they come to see me marry?
I shall throw my bride right into the sea,
If they are not here by half-past three."
But the belle was laughing, " Oh, what shall we do!"
And the beaux were crying, " Bee·bee-bee-boo."

THE CHILDREN AND THE GARLAND.

"TO-MORROW is May-day," the children said; "the birds must call us very early, and we will go to the woods and make a garland." And in the morning, long before the sun had looked over the tops of the houses into the village street, they were far away in the woods.

"I will give them some roses as they come back," the gardener said. "They shall put them among the spring flowers, as a swallow among the thrushes, to show that summer is on its way."

When the children had made their garland and a posy for each one of them, they went singing all down the village street, over the grey stone bridge, beyond the hayricks, and past the houses on the hill-side.

In one of the houses there was a pale little child with a sad, thin face. "Mother," he said, "here are some children with a garland. Will it be summer when they have gone by?" He called after them as they went on, "Come back, oh, come back again!"

"Yes, we will come back," they answered, but they went on their way singing. All through the day he waited for them, but they did not come; and at last, when it was evening, the mother took him up into her arms to carry him to his bed. Suddenly he heard the children singing in the distance. "Oh, mother," he exclaimed, "they are coming;" and he watched till they came up the hill again and stood before him. "But where is your garland?" he asked.

"We gave it to lame Mary, the postman's wife, for she is always longing to see the fields," they answered; "but these roses are for you, dear little boy; they are all for you," and putting them into his hands they went back to the village.

"You are very tired," the child said to the roses; "all your leaves are drooping. Poor roses, perhaps you are lonely away from the garden; but you shall sleep near me, and there is a star rising up in the sky; it will watch us all through the night." Then the child nestled down in his white bed—he and his little warm heart, in which there was love for all things. While he slept the roses looked at his pale little face and sighed, and presently they stole softly on to his cheeks and rested there. The children saw them still there when the summer was over; when the garland was quite dead, and lame Mary longed for the fields no more.

ROUND THE TEA-TABLE.

A NICE little party we're seated at tea,
   The dollies all seem very glad,
Save the poor little thing who is leaning on me ;
   I fear that she feels rather bad ;
Poor limp little thing ! she wants a back-bone,
   She's only just made up of rag.
There's little Miss Prim sitting up all alone,
   And the Japanese looks like a wag.

Now what shall we talk of, my own dollies fair ?
   And what shall we give you for tea ?
That queer little thing with the short frizzy hair,
   Why does he keep looking at me ?
My sister and I we will sing you a song
   Before we get up from the table ;
It shall not be sad, and it shall not be long—
   We'll sing it as well as we're able.

SONG.

The darkness is stealing all over the place,
   The flowers are weeping for sorrow,
The daisy is hiding its little round face,
   The sun has gone seeking to-morrow.

So while you are seated all round the tea-table,
Please join in the chorus as well as you're able ;
  O ! sing ! sing away for your life.

CHORUS.

It's time to cut off the dicky birds' noses,
Time to cut off the dicky birds' noses,
It's time to cut off the dicky birds' noses,
  So bring me the carving-knife.

The darkness is hiding the birds on the trees,
  The thrushes are weary of singing,
A strange little rumour is borne on the breeze
  Of Summer the swallows are bringing.

So while you are seated all round the tea-table,
Please join in the chorus as well as you're able ;
  O ! sing ! sing away for your life.

CHORUS.

It's time to cut off the dicky birds' noses,
Time to cut off the dicky birds' noses,
It's time to cut off the dicky birds' noses,
  So bring me the carving-knife.

The Summer is stealing all over the place,
  The wind is all scented with roses,
The dear little birds are all flying a race,
  On purpose to give us their noses.

5

So while you are seated all round the tea-table,
Please join in the chorus as well as you're able ;
O ! sing ! sing away for your life.

CHORUS.

It's time to cut off the dicky birds' noses
Time to cut off the dicky birds' noses,
It's time to cut off the dicky birds' noses,
So bring me the carving-knife.

TOMMY.

TOMMY was sitting on the bench near the end of the lane. By his side was a basin tied up in a cotton handkerchief; in the button-hole of his coat there was a sprig of sweet-william. The girls from the big house came and stood still in front of him, staring at him rudely, but he did not speak.

"Tommy, are you tired?" they asked.

"Yes," Tommy answered, crossly, "I'm very tired, and father's working in the fields, and I have got to take him his dinner before I go to the fair."

"Why don't the servants take it?"

"Servants!" said Tommy scornfully; "we've no servants. We are not rich people!"

"Wouldn't you like to be rich?" the eldest sister asked, while the two little ones walked slowly round Tommy, looking at the feather in his hat; he had put it there so that he might look smart when he went on to the village.

"No, it's too expensive," said Tommy, shaking his head; "rich people have to buy such a lot of things, and to wear fine clothes, and they can't have dinner in the fields."

"My father has his dinner in a room," said the girl.

"That's because he's rich," answered Tommy, "and people would talk if he didn't ; rich people can't do as they like, as poor can."

"And my father lives in a big house," the girl went on, for she was vulgar, and liked to boast.

"Yes, and it takes up a lot of room ; my father's got the whole world to live in if he likes ; that's better than a house."

"But my father doesn't work," said the girl, scornfully.

"Mine does," said Tommy, proudly. "Rich people can't work," he went on, "so they are obliged to get the poor folk to do it. Why, we have made everything in the world. Oh ! it's a fine thing to be poor."

"But suppose all the rich folk died, what would the poor folk do ?"

"But suppose all the poor folk died," cried Tommy, "what would the rich folk do ? They can sit in carriages, but can't build them, and eat dinners, but can't cook them." And he got up and went his way. "Poor folk ought to be very kind to rich folk, for it's hard to be the like of them," he said to himself as he went along.

THE SWALLOWS.

THERE were some children in the north looking at the swallows flying south. "Why are
they going away?" the little one asked.

"The summer is over," the elder sister answered,
"and if they stayed here they would be starved and
die of cold, and so, when the summer goes, they
journey south."

"Our mother and sisters are in the south," the
little one said, as they looked after the birds.
"Dear little swallows, tell mother that we are
watching for her!" But they were already flying
over the sea. The chilly winds tried to follow, but
the swallows flew so swiftly they were not over-
taken; they went on, with the summer always
before them. They were tired many a time; once
they stayed to rest upon the French coast, and
once, in the Bay of Biscay, they clung to the rigging
of a ship all through the night, but in the morning
they went on again.

Far away in the south, two English children were
looking from the turret window of an old castle.

"Here are the swallows," they said; "perhaps
they have come from England. Dear swallows,
have you brought us a message?" they asked.

"It was very cold, we had no time for messages;

and we must not lose the track of summer," the swallows twittered, and they flew on till they reached the African shore.

"Poor little swallows," said the English children, as they watched the ship come into port that was to take them back to their own land ; "they have to chase the summer and the sun, but we do not mind whether it is summer or winter, for if we only keep our hearts warm, the rest does not matter."

"It is very good of the swallows to come to us," the elder sister said, in the next spring, when she heard their first soft twitter beneath the eaves, "for the summer is in many places, and we are so far from the south."

"Yes, it is very good of them to come," the children answered ; "dear little swallows, perhaps they love us !"

A FIRST LOVE-MAKING.

A LAND there is beyond the sea
   That I have never seen,
But Johnny says he'll take me there,
   And I shall be a queen.
He'll build for me a palace there,
   Its roof will be of thatch,
And it will have a little porch
   And everything to match.

And he'll give me a garden-green,
   And he'll give me a crown
Of flowers that love the wood and field
   And never grow in town.
And we shall be so happy there,
   And never, never part,
And I shall be the grandest queen—
   The queen of Johnny's heart.

Then, Johnny, man your little boat
   To sail across the sea ;
There's only room for king and queen—
   For Johnny and for me.
And, Johnny dear, I'm not afraid
   Of any wind or tide,
For I am always safe, my dear,
   If you are by my side.

SMUT.

NOW, this story is quite true. Once upon a time there was a cat called Mr. Puff; he lived in a grand house, quite close to the Turkish Embassy. A lord and a lady and several servants lived with Mr. Puff; he was very kind to them, letting them do in all things as they liked, and never sending them away or keeping the house to himself. One day Mr. Puff, being out in the rain, found a poor little kitten, covered with mud, and crying bitterly: so Mr. Puff took the kitten between his teeth, carried it home, and set it down on the drawing-room hearth-rug. The lord and the lady had the kitten washed, and gave it food, and called it Smut. Then Smut went and sat him down on the lord's writing-table.

When Smut grew to be a cat, but before he was yet a large one, the lord and the lady thought awhile, and spoke, "We have a dear friend," they said, "and he is catless; therefore, if Mr. Puff will agree, we will take Smut to him as a present." And Mr. Puff agreed. So Smut was put into a birdcage, for there was nothing else to serve him for a travelling carriage, and taken to the dear friend's house. The dear friend had a little girl with golden hair, and when she saw Smut, she cried out for joy, and said, " Never before did I see a dicky-bird with a furry coat, a long tail, and little white teeth." But Smut shook his head, as if to say, " I am not a dicky-bird, sweet maid, but only a four-legged cat ;" then they opened the birdcage door, and he walked out, waving his tail.

Now, when Smut grew up, his gravity and dignity made all who knew his history wonder, and few could believe that he had once been a dirty kitten, covered with mud, glad to accept the charity of Mr. Puff. When a year had gone, or perhaps even a longer time, there was a great war in Turkey, and terrible battles were fought. Then Smut looked very anxious, and went quite bald, and his coat fell off in little patches ; but none could tell why. At last he died, and the little girl wept sorely, and all who had known him grieved and lamented.

And when Smut had been sleeping only a little while beneath the lilac tree, accident revealed that, instead of a lowly foundling, he had been of high degree, for the little vagrant Mr. Puff had found was no less a person than the Turkish Ambassador's coachman's wife's cat's kitten.

SEE-SAW.

GET into the boat and away to the west,
        See-saw ! see-saw !
For they've cut down the tree with the poor linnet's
    nest,
        See-saw ! see-saw !
The bulrushes nod and the water-lilies sigh,
        See-saw ! see-saw !
And all of us know the sad reason why,
        See-saw ! see-saw !

    For, oh ! the tree—the tree's cut down,
    And every one of its leaves are brown ;
    And in the field the children play,
    But the little linnet has flown away :
        Oh, dear ! oh, dear ! oh, dear !

THE BAD GIRL.

SHE was always called the bad girl, for she had once, when she was very little, put out her tongue at the postman. She lived alone with her grandmother and her three brothers in the cottage beyond the field, and the girls in the village took no notice of her. The bad girl did not mind this, for she was always thinking of the cuckoo clock. The clock stood in one corner of the cottage, and every hour a door opened at the top of its face, and a little cuckoo came out and called its name just the same number of times that the clock ought to have struck, and called it so loudly and in so much haste that the clock was afraid to strike at all. The bad girl was always wondering whether it was worse for the clock to have a cupboard in its forehead, and a bird that was always hopping in and out, or for the poor cuckoo to spend so much time in a dark little prison. "If it could only get away to the woods," she said to herself, " who knows but its voice might grow sweet, and even life itself might come to it !" She thought of the clock so much that her grand-mother used to say—

"Ah, lassie, if you would only think of me some-times !" But the bad girl would answer—

"You are not in prison, granny dear, and you

have not even a bee in your bonnet, let alone a bird in your head. Why should I think of you?"

One day, close by the farm, she saw the big girls from the school gathering flowers.

"Give me one," she said; "perhaps the cuckoo would like it." But they all cried, "No, no!" and tried to frighten her away. "They are for the little one's birthday. To-morrow she will be seven years old," they said, "and she is to have a crown of flowers and a cake, and all the afternoon we shall play merry games with her."

"Is she unhappy, that you are taking so much trouble for her?" asked the bad girl.

"Oh, no; she is very happy: but it will be her birthday, and we want to make her happier."

"Why?"

"Because we love her," said one;

"Because she is so little," said another;

"Because she is alive," said a third.

"Are all things that live to be loved and cared for?" the bad girl asked, but they were too busy to listen, so she went on her way thinking; and it seemed as if all things round—the birds, and bees, and the rustling leaves, and the little tender wild flowers, half hidden in the grass—answered, as she went along—

"Yes, they are all to be cared for and made happier, if it be possible."

"The cuckoo clock is not alive," she thought.

"Oh, no ; it is not alive," the trees answered ; "but many things that do not live have voices, and many others are just sign-posts, pointing the way."

"The way ! The way to what, and where ?"

"We find out for ourselves ;—we must all find out for ourselves," the trees sighed and whispered to each other.

As the bad girl entered the cottage, the cuckoo called out its name eleven times, but she did not even look up. She walked straight across to the chair by the fireside, and kneeling down, kissed her granny's hands.

MORNING TIME.

I.

AWAKE, my pet !
What ! slumbering yet,
When the day's so warm and bright ?
The flowers that wept
Before they slept
O'er the darkness of yesternight,
Have listened long
To the lark's wild song,
And awoke with the morning light.

II.

Again and again
Through the window-pane
The jasmine flowers kept peeping,
And in at the door,
And along the floor,
The sunny rays came creeping,
So I opened wide
The sash, and tried
To tell them you were sleeping.

III.

Awake, my dear,
The winter drear
Has fled with all things dreary,
But quickly by
The spring will fly,
And soon the birds will weary.—
Awake while yet
The dew is wet
And day is young, my deary.

THE PINK PARASOL.

THE pink parasol had tender whalebone ribs and a slender stick of cherry-wood. It lived with the wilful child in the white-house, just beyond the third milestone. All about the trees were green, and the flowers grew tall; in the pond behind the willows the ducks swam round and round and dipped their heads beneath the water.

Every bird and bee, every leaf and flower, loved the child and the pink parasol as they wandered in the garden together, listening to the birds and seeking the shady spots to rest in, or walking up and down the long trim pathway in the sunshine. Yet the child tired of it all, and before the summer was over, was always standing by the gate, watching the straight white road that stretched across the plain.

"If I might but see the city, with the busy streets and the eager crowds," he was always saying to himself.

Then all that lived in the garden knew that the child would not be with them long. At last the day came when he flung down the pink parasol, and, without even one last look at the garden, ran out at the gate.

The flowers died, and the swallows journeyed

south ; the trees stretched higher and higher, to see the child come back across the plain, but he never came. "Ah, dear child!" they sighed many a time, "why are you staying? and are your eyes as blue as ever; or have the sad tears dimmed them? and is your hair golden still? and your voice, is it like the singing of the birds? And your heart—oh! my dear, my dear, what is in your heart now, that once was so full of summer and the sun?"

The pink parasol lay on the pathway, where the child left it, spoilt by the rain, and splashed by the gravel, faded and forgotten. At last, a gipsy lad, with dark eyes, a freckled face, and little gold rings in his ears, came by; he picked up the pink parasol, hid it under his coat, and carried it to the gipsy tent. There it stayed till one day the cherry-wood stick was broken into three pieces, and the pink parasol was put on the fire to make the water boil for the gipsy's tea.

THE SISTERS.

THE little sisters went into the room to play at ball.

"We must be careful not to wake the white cat," the tall one said, softly.

"Or to spoil the roses," the fat one whispered; "but throw high, dear sister, or we shall never hit the ceiling."

"You dear children," thought the white cat, "why do you come to play here at all? Only just round the corner are the shady trees, and the birds singing on the branches, and the sunshine is flecking the pathway. Who knows but what, out there, your ball might touch the sky? Here you will only disturb me, and perhaps spoil the roses; and at best you can but hit the ceiling !"

THE WHITE RABBITS.

ALL the white rabbits but two, my dears,
　All the white rabbits but two,
Away they all sailed in a cockle-shell boat,
　Painted a beautiful blue.

All the white rabbits so snowy and sleek,
　Away they went down to the shore ;
Little they thought, so happy and meek,
　They'd never come up from it more.

Oh, the white rabbits they wept and they sobbed,
　Till the boat it shook up in the sails ;
Oh, the white rabbits they sobbed and they shook
　From their poor loppy ears to their tails.

Away they all sailed to a desolate land
　Where never a lettuce-leaf grew,
All the white rabbits but two, my dears,
　All tho white rabbits but two.

THE WOODEN HORSE.

"COME and have a ride," the big brother said.
"I am afraid," the little one answered;
"the horse's mouth is wide open."

"But it's only wooden. That is the best of a horse that isn't real. If his mouth is ever so wide open, he cannot shut it. So come," and the big brother lifted the little one up, and dragged him about.

"Oh, do stop!" the little one cried out in terror; "does the horse make that noise along the floor?"

"Yes."

"And is it a real noise?"

"Of course it is," the big brother answered.

"But I thought only real things could make real things," the little one said; "where does the imitation horse end and the real sound begin?"

At this the big brother stood still for a few minutes.

"I was thinking about real and imitation things," he said presently. "It's very difficult to tell which is which sometimes. You see they get so close together that the one often grows into the other, and some imitated things become real and some real ones become imitation as they go on. But I should say that you are a real coward for not having a ride."

"No, I am not," the little one laughed ; and, getting astride the wooden horse, he sat up bravely. "Oh, Jack, dear," he said to his brother, " we will always be glad that we are real boys, or we too might have been made with mouths we were never able to shut ! "

THE DUCK POND.

SO little Bridget took the baby on her right arm and a jug in her left hand, and went to the farm to get the milk. On her way she went by the garden-gate of a large house that stood close to the farm, and she told the baby a story :—

"Last summer," she said, "a little girl, bigger than you, for she was just able to walk, came to stay in that house—she and her father and mother. All about the road just here, the ducks and the chickens from the farm, and an old turkey, used to walk about all the day long, but the poor little ducks were very unhappy, for they had no pond to swim about in, only that narrow ditch through which the streamlet is flowing. When the little girl's father saw this, he took a spade, and worked and worked very hard, and out of the ditch and the streamlet he made a little pond for the ducks, and they swam about and were very happy all through the summer days. Every morning I used to stand and watch, and presently the garden-gate would open, and then the father would come out, leading the little girl by the hand, and the mother brought a large plateful of bits of broken bread. The little girl used to throw the bread to the ducks, and they ran after it and ate it up quickly, while she laughed out with glee, and the father and the mother laughed too just as merrily. Baby, the father had blue eyes, and a voice that you seemed to hear with your heart.

"The little girl used to feed the chickens too, and the foolish old turkey that was so fond of her it would run after her until she screamed and was afraid. The dear father and the little girl came out every morning, while the black pigs looked through the bars of the farm-yard gate and grunted at them, as if they were glad, and I think the ducks knew that the father had made the pond, for they swam round and round it proudly while he watched them, but when he went away they seemed tired and sad.

"The pond is not there now, baby, for a man came by one day and made it into a ditch again; and the chickens and the ducks from the farm are kept in another place.

"The little girl is far away in her own home, which the father made for her, and the dear father lives in his own home too—in the hearts of those he loved."

That was the story that Bridget told the baby.

THE LITTLE MAID.

THERE is a sweet maiden asleep by the sea,
    Her lips are as red as a cherry ;
The roses are resting upon her brown cheeks—
    Her cheeks that are brown as a berry.

She's tired of building up castles of sand,
    Her hands they are gritty and grubby ;
Her shoes, they are wet, and her legs, they are bare,
    Her legs that are sturdy and chubby.

I'll wrap a shawl round you, my dear little maid,
    To keep the wind off you completely,
And soft I will sing you a lullaby song,
    And soon you will slumber most sweetly.

THE DONKEY ON WHEELS.

THERE was once a poor little donkey on wheels. It had never wagged its tail, or tossed its head, or said, "Hee-haw!" or tasted a tender thistle. It always went about, anywhere that anyone pulled it, on four wooden wheels, carrying a foolish knight, who wore a large cocked hat and a long cloak, because he had no legs. Now, a man who has no legs, and rides a donkey on wheels, has little cause for pride ; but the knight was haughty, and seldom remembered his circumstances. So the donkey suffered sorely, and in many ways.

One day the donkey and the knight were on the table in front of the child to whom they both belonged. She was cutting out a little doll's frock with a large pair of scissors.

"Mistress," said the knight, "this donkey tries my temper. Will you give me some spurs?"

"Oh, no, sir knight," the child answered. "You would hurt the poor donkey ; besides, you have no heels to put them on."

"Cruel knight!" exclaimed the donkey. "Make him get off, dear mistress ; I will carry him no longer."

"Let him stay," said the child, gently ; "he has no legs, and cannot walk."

"Then why did he want spurs?"

"Just the way of the world, dear donkey; just the way of the world."

"Ah!" sighed the donkey, "some ways are very trying, especially the world's;" and then it said no more, but thought of the fields it would never see, and the thistles it would never taste.

COCK-A-DOODLE.

I KNOW a lovely dicky-bird,
   A cock-a-doodle-doo ;—
My father and my mother
   And my sister know it too.

It struts about so gaily,
   And it is brave and strong ;
And when it crows, it is a crow,
   Both very loud and long.

Oh, " Cock-a-doodle-doo," it crows,
   And cock-a-doodle won't
Leave off its cock-a-doodling,
   When mother dear cries " Don't ! "

THE BOY AND LITTLE GREAT LADY.

SHE was always called the "little great lady," for she lived in a grand house, and was very rich. He was a strange boy; the little great lady never knew whence he came, or whither he went. She only saw him when the snow lay deep upon the ground. Then in the early morning he swept a pathway to the stable in which she had once kept a white rabbit. When it was quite finished, she came down the steps in her white dress and little thin shoes, with bows on them, and walked slowly along the pathway. It was always swept so dry she might have worn paper shoes without getting them wet. At the far end he always stood waiting till she came, and smiled and said, "Thank you, little boy," and passed on. Then he was no more seen till the next snowy morning, when again he swept the pathway ; and again the little great lady came down the steps in her dainty shoes, and went on her way to the stable.

But at last, one morning when the snow lay white and thick, and she came down the steps as usual, there was no pathway. The little boy stood leaning on a spade, his feet buried deep in the snow.

"Where is your broom ? and where is the pathway to the rabbit house ? " she asked.

"The rabbit is dead, and the broom is worn out," he answered; "and I am tired of making pathways that lead to empty houses."

"But why have you done it so long?" she asked.

"You have bows on your shoes," he said; "and they are so thin you could not walk over the snow in them—why, you would catch your death of cold," he added, scornfully.

"What would you do if I wore boots?"

"I should go and learn how to build ships, or paint pictures, or write books. But I should not think of you so much," he said.

The little great lady answered eagerly, "Go and learn how to do all those things; I will wait till you come back and tell me what you have done," and she turned and went into the house.

"Good-bye," the boy said, as he stood watching for a moment the closed door; "dear little great lady, good-bye." And he went along the unmade pathway beyond the empty rabbit house.

GOOD-DAY, GENTLE FOLK.

OH, yes, sir and miss, I have been to the
    town ;
    It really was pleasant and gay ;
But now I must hurry, the sun's going down,
    And so I will wish you good-day.
And so I will wish you good-day, gentle folk,
    And so I will wish you good-day.

I know a white rabbit just over the hill,
    He's eating a lettuce for tea ;
And a fat speckled duck, with a very large bill,
    Is quacking, " Oh, where can she be?"
And two little mice are there, standing quite still,
    They're all of them waiting for me.

For we all love the stars and the little pale moon,
    Beneath them we frolic and play ;
My friends have been waiting the whole afternoon,
    And so I will wish you good-day.
And so I will wish you good-day, gentle folk,
    And so I will wish you good-day.